OLD
MACDONALD
Had a Farm
AND OTHER
Animal Nursery Rhymes

Published by Bonney Press,
an imprint of Hinkler Books Pty Ltd
45–55 Fairchild Street
Heatherton Victoria 3202 Australia
www.hinkler.com.au

BONNEY PRESS

Illustrators: Steph Baxter, Sarah Coleman, Jon Contino, Sarah Dennis, Lauren Hom, Lalalimola, Mick Marston, Jess Matthews, Marie Simpson, Alice Stevenson, Chris Robertson, Yulia Vysotskaya.

ISBN: 978 1 4889 0041 9

Printed and bound in China

Contents

Old MacDonald had a farm, E-I-E-I-O!
And on that farm he had a cow, E-I-E-I-O!
With a moo moo here and a moo moo there,
Here a moo, there a moo,
Everywhere a moo moo!
Old MacDonald had a farm, E-I-E-I-O!

Old MacDonald had a farm, E-I-E-I-O!
And on that farm he had a pig, E-I-E-I-O!
With an oink oink here and an oink oink there...

Old MacDonald had a farm, E-I-E-I-O!
And on that farm he had a horse, E-I-E-I-O!
With a neigh neigh here and a neigh neigh there...

Old MacDonald had a farm, E-I-E-I-O!
And on that farm he had a duck, E-I-E-I-O!
With a quack quack here and a quack quack there...

Old MacDonald had a farm, E-I-E-I-O!
And on that farm he had a dog, E-I-E-I-O!
With a woof woof here and a woof woof there...

BAA, BAA, BLACK SHEEP,
HAVE YOU ANY WOOL?
YES, SIR, YES, SIR,
THREE BAGS
FULL.

One for the master,
and one for the dame,
and one for the little boy
who lives down
the lane.

Old Mother Hubbard
Went to the cupboard
To fetch her poor dog a bone;
When she got there,
The cupboard was bare,
And so the poor dog had none.

She went to the baker's
To buy him some bread;
But when she came back,
The poor dog was dead!

She went to the undertaker's
To buy him a coffin;
But when she came back,
The poor dog was laughing.

She went to the fishmonger's
To buy him some fish;
But when she came back,
He was washing the dish.

She went to the hatter's
To buy him a hat;
But when she came back,
He was feeding her cat.

She went to the barber's
To buy him a wig;
But when she came back,
He was dancing a jig.

She went to the fruiterer's
To buy him some fruit;
But when she came back,
He was playing the flute.

She went to the tailor's
To buy him a coat;
But when she came back,
He was riding a goat.

She went to the cobbler's
To buy him some shoes;
But when she came back,
He was reading the news.

She went to the seamstress
To buy him some linen;
But when she came back,
The dog was a-spinning.

She went to the hosier's
To buy him some hose;
But when she came back,
He was dressed in his clothes.

The dame made a curtsy,
The dog made a bow;
The dame said, 'Your servant!'
The dog said, 'Bow-wow!'

Ding, dong, bell,
Pussy's in the well.
Who put her in?
Little JOHNNY GREEN.
Who pulled her out?
Little TOMMY STOUT.
What a naughty boy was that,
To try and drown poor pussy cat,
Who never did him any harm,
And killed the mice
in his
father's
barn.

Hickety, pickety, my black hen,
She lays eggs for gentlemen;
Gentlemen come every day
To see what my black hen doth lay;
Sometimes nine and sometimes ten,
Hickety, pickety, my black hen.

Hickory, dickory, dock,
The mouse ran up the clock,
The clock struck one,
The mouse ran down,
Hickory, dickory, dock.

Pussycat, pussycat, where have you been?
I've been to London to visit the queen.
Pussycat, pussycat, what did you there?
I frightened a little mouse under her chair.

MARY HAD A LITTLE
LAMB
ITS FLEECE
WAS WHITE AS SNOW
AND everywhere THAT MARY WENT
THE LAMB WAS Sure TO GO
IT FOLLOWED HER TO SCHOOL
ONE DAY
WHICH WAS AGAINST
the rule
IT MADE THE CHILDREN
LAUGH AND PLAY
TO SEE A Lamb AT SCHOOL!

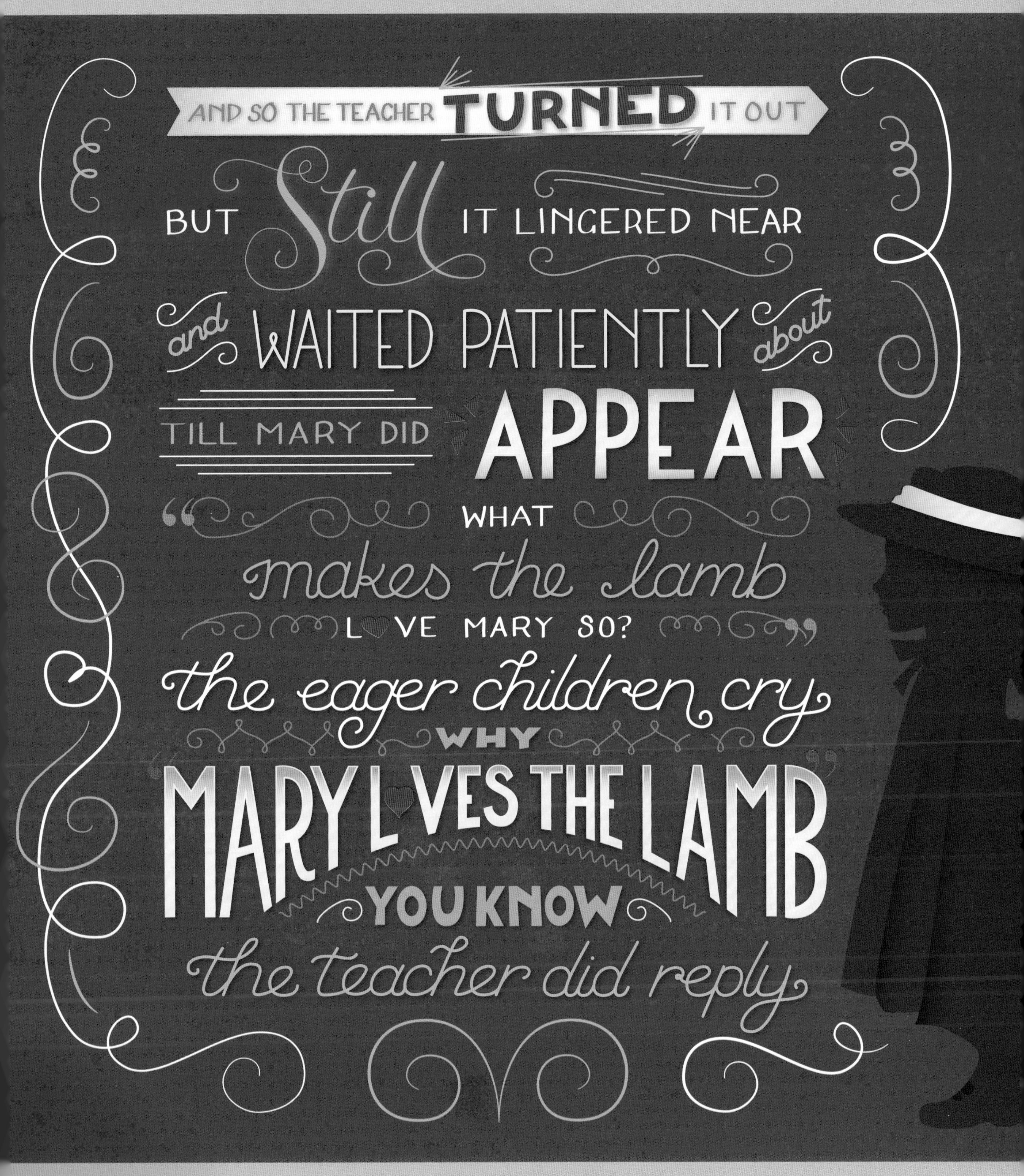
AND SO THE TEACHER TURNED IT OUT
BUT Still IT LINGERED NEAR
and WAITED PATIENTLY about
TILL MARY DID APPEAR
"WHAT
makes the lamb
LOVE MARY SO?"
the eager children cry
WHY
"MARY LOVES THE LAMB
YOU KNOW"
the teacher did reply

The Owl and the Pussycat went to sea
In a beautiful pea-green boat;
They took some honey, and plenty of money,
Wrapped up in a five-pound note.
The Owl looked up to the stars above,
And sang to a small guitar,
'O lovely Pussy! O Pussy, my love,
What a beautiful Pussy you are,
You are, you are!
What a beautiful Pussy you are!'

Pussy said to the Owl, 'You elegant fowl!
How charmingly sweet you sing!
O, let us be married; too long we have tarried:
But what shall we do for a ring?'
They sailed away, for a year and a day,
To the land where the bong-tree grows
And there in a wood a Piggy-wig stood,
With a ring at the end of his nose,
His nose, his nose,
With a ring at the end of his nose.

'Dear Pig, are you willing to sell for one shilling
Your ring?' Said the Piggy, 'I will.'
So they took it away, and were married next day
By the turkey who lives on the hill.
They dined on mince and slices of quince,
Which they ate with a runcible spoon;
And hand in hand, on the edge of the sand,
They danced by the light of the moon,
The moon, the moon,
They danced by the light of the moon.

ONCE I SAW A little bird
COME HOP hop HOP
So I cried, "LITTLE BIRD
WILL YOU STOP stop STOP?"
I WAS going TO THE window,
To say "HOW DO YOU DO?"
BUT HE shook HIS little TAIL,
And far away he flew.

Ride a cock-horse to Banbury Cross,
To see a fine lady upon a white horse;
With rings on her fingers and bells on her toes,
She shall have music wherever she goes.

I love little pussy,
Her coat is so warm,
And if I don't hurt her,
She'll do me no harm.

So I'll not pull her tail,
Nor drive her away,
But pussy and I,
Together will play.

WHAT DO YOU SUPPOSE?
A BEE SAT ON MY NOSE.
THEN WHAT DO YOU THINK?
HE GAVE ME A WINK
AND SAID,
"I BEG YOUR PARDON,
I THOUGHT YOU WERE
THE GARDEN!"

Three little kittens, they lost their mittens,
And they began to cry;
Oh, mother dear, we sadly fear
That we have lost our mittens.
What! Lost your mittens, you naughty kittens!
Then you shall have no pie.
Mee-ow, mee-ow, mee-ow,
No, you shall have no pie.

The three little kittens, they found their mittens,
And they began to cry;
Oh, mother dear, see here, see here,
For we have found our mittens.
Put on your mittens, you silly kittens,
And you shall have some pie.
Purr-r, purr-r, purr-r,
Oh, let us have some pie.

The three little kittens put on their mittens,
And soon ate up the pie;
Oh, mother dear, we greatly fear
That we have soiled our mittens.
What! Soiled your mittens, you naughty kittens!
Then they began to sigh,
Mee-ow, mee-ow, mee-ow,
Then they began to sigh.

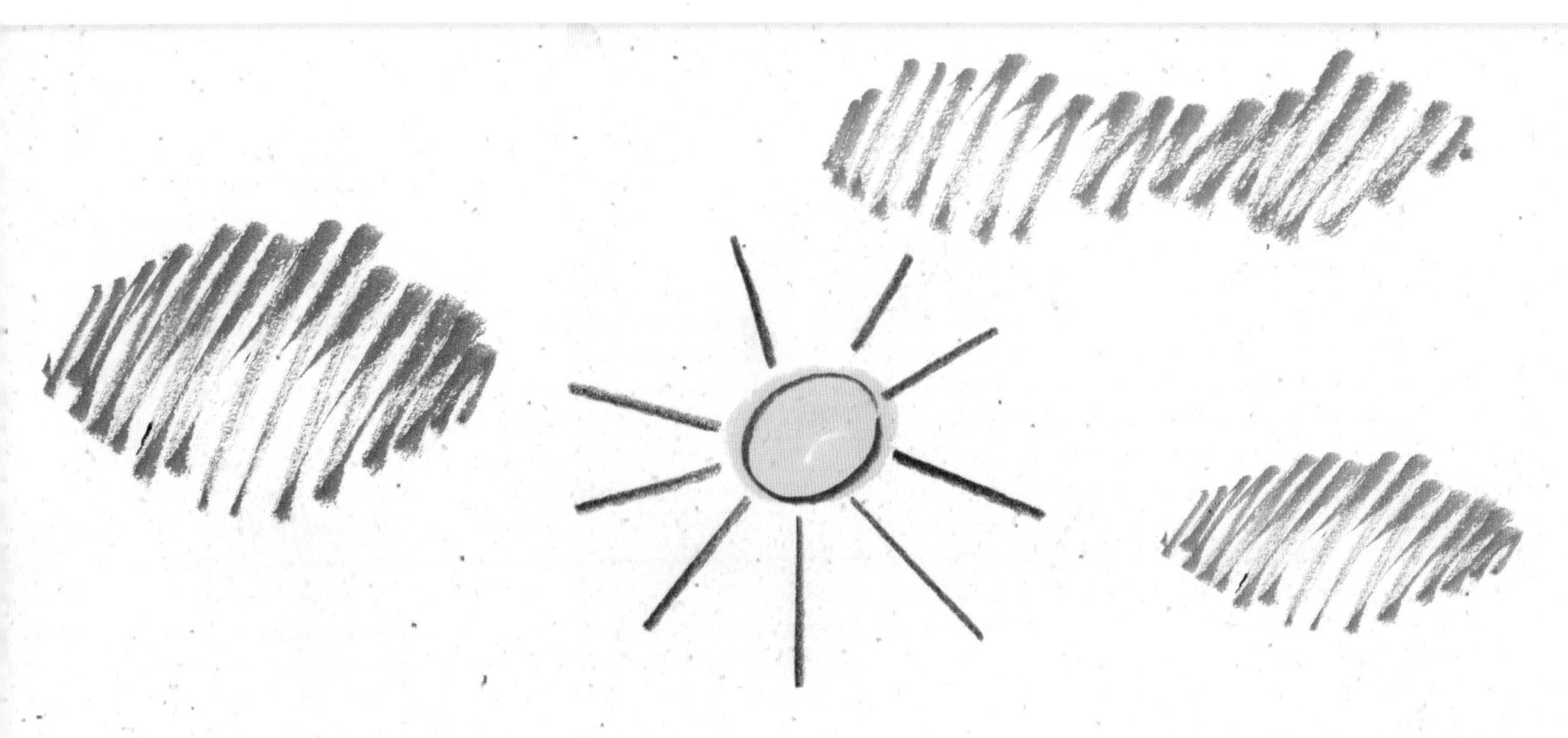

The three little kittens, they washed their mittens,
And hung them out to dry;
Oh, mother dear, do you not hear,
That we have washed our mittens?
What! Washed your mittens, you good little kittens,
But I smell a rat close by.
Mee-ow, mee-ow, mee-ow,
We smell a rat close by.

HIGGLETY
PIGGLETY POP!
THE DOG HAS EATEN THE MOP
THE PIG'S IN A HURRY
THE CAT'S
in a flurry
HIGGLETY
PIGGLETY
POP!